Robert Lee

History of the Discoveries of the Circulation of the Blood

of the ganglia and nerves, and of the action of the heart

Robert Lee

History of the Discoveries of the Circulation of the Blood
of the ganglia and nerves, and of the action of the heart

ISBN/EAN: 9783337393014

Printed in Europe, USA, Canada, Australia, Japan

Cover: Foto ©Andreas Hilbeck / pixelio.de

More available books at **www.hansebooks.com**

HISTORY OF THE DISCOVERIES

OF THE

CIRCULATION OF THE BLOOD,

OF THE

GANGLIA AND NERVES,

AND OF THE

ACTION OF THE HEART.

BY

ROBERT LEE, M.D. F.R.S.

LONDON:

RICHARD BENTLEY, NEW BURLINGTON STREET,

Publisher in Ordinary to Her Majesty.

1865.

c/

INTRODUCTION.

ERASISTRATUS and Herophilus considered the brain, spinal cord, and nerves to be the primary organs of sensation and motion. Galen affirmed that the brain is the origin of the nerves, and that there is no part of the animal frame endowed with sensation and voluntary motion which does not possess nerves, and that if a nerve be cut, the part which it had supplied is immediately deprived of sensation and motion. Galen first described the ganglia of the great Sympathetic nerve, respecting which he says, "Est autem et aliud mirabile naturæ ab anatomicis ignoratum." This wonderful work of nature of which anatomists were ignorant before the time of Galen, appears to have fallen into oblivion until many ages had elapsed after his death, when these ganglia were again described by Fallopius, and called corpora olivaria.

Ganglia have since been discovered on other nerves besides the great Sympathetic, especially on the Fifth pair, and the posterior roots of the spinal nerves; and it is now known to all anatomists that there are numerous tribes of living creatures endowed with sensation and power of motion, which have neither brain nor spinal marrow, whose whole nervous system consists of ganglia and nerves. Numerous treatises on the structure and functions of ganglia and nerves were published by foreign anatomists between 1791 and 1795, but their opinions were conjectural and discordant. Microscopical researches have since been made upon this subject, without any satisfactory results.

If the engravings of Scarpa and Swan be examined, it will be seen that only a few small branches of nerves have been represented passing into the substance of the heart, lungs, œsophagus, stomach, alimentary canal, liver, pancreas, spleen, kidneys, uterus, and bladder. Nerves had in fact been traced by these and other anatomists to the viscera of the thorax, abdomen, and pelvis, but not into their substance or parenchymatous structure, at least not to any considerable extent; and it was long maintained by many eminent anatomists, and is still asserted by some, that the functions of the internal organs of the body do not depend upon nervous influence, and that these organs are sparingly endowed with nervous structures. It does not appear that any of the distinguished anatomists who flourished before the middle of the present century ever suspected that there exists a great system of ganglia and nerves distributed throughout the substance of the several internal organs of the body, and that to the influence of these ganglia and nerves the functions of circulation, respiration, digestion, secretion, and parturition might be referred.

In a paper which I presented to the Royal Society in 1839, entitled, "On the Nerves of the Gravid Uterus," I described four great plexures under the peritoneum of the grand uterus, which had an extensive connexion with the hypogastric, spermatic, and sacral nerves. From their form, colour, and general distribution, and their resemblance to ganglionic plexures of nerves, and from their branches actually coalescing and being continuous with the hypogastric, sacral, and spermatic nerves, I was induced to believe, on first discovering them, that they were nervous ganglionic plexuses, and constituted the special nervous system of the uterus.

The two Referees appointed by the Council to examine the Paper quickly decided, without any sufficient investigation with the microscope, that the structures I had discovered were not Nerves, and the Paper was immediately withdrawn from the Royal Society. The investigation was continued with increased vigour.

On the 1st January, 1841, "The Anatomy of the Nerves of the Uterus," with three engravings, was published, in which I described ten dissections which I had made of the Ganglia and Nerves of the Unimpregnated and Gravid Uterus.

In a paper "On the Nervous Ganglia of the Uterus," published with two engravings in the Philosophical Transactions for 1841, I stated, as the result of dissections I had made of the unimpregnated uterus, and of the gravid uterus in the third, fourth, sixth, seventh, and ninth months of pregnancy, that there are many large ganglia on the uterine nerves, and on those of the vagina and bladder, which increase with the coats, blood-vessels, and absorbents of the uterus during pregnancy, and which return after parturition to their original condition before conception takes place.

In an Appendix to this paper, published in the Philosophical Transactions for 1842, with an engraving, I described and delineated two great ganglia on the sides of the neck of the uterus, in which the hypogastric and spinal nerves terminate, and from which numerous nerves proceed to the uterus, vagina, bladder, and rectum. Other ganglia and nerves were described and delineated, which were situated under the peritoneum of the body of the uterus. "These dissections prove," I observed, "that the human uterus possesses a great system of nerves, which enlarges with the coats, blood-vessels, and absorbents during pregnancy, and which returns after parturition to its original condition before conception takes place. It is chiefly by the influence of these ganglia and nerves that the uterus performs the varied functions of menstruation, conception, and parturition, and it is solely by their means that the whole fabric of the nervous system sympathizes with the different morbid affections of the uterus. If these ganglia and nerves of the uterus could not be demonstrated, its physiology and pathology would be completely inexplicable."

In the "Memoirs on the Ganglia and Nerves of the Uterus," published by me in 1849, I have given a correct history of

B

all the proceedings which took place in the Council and Committee of Physiology of the Royal Society in 1845, the effect of which was, for a time, to induce many anatomists and physiologists, who had never dissected the parts, to believe that the ganglia and other nervous structures of the uterus, which were described and delineated by me in the Philosophical Transactions, had no existence in nature, but had been fabricated from elastic tissue, cellular membrane, or muscular fibres. The illegal award of the Royal Medal in Physiology to a person, who had mutilated the structures in two preparations, by the clandestine removal of one of the constituent tissues of the ganglia and nerves, the neurilemma, contributed powerfully to the same effect.

The evil consequences of such acts to science, morality, and sound practical principles, were incalculable, but they were only temporary; and out of this darkness and prejudice speedily sprung the Ganglia and Nerves of the Heart, which were destined to encounter the same blind opposition from the same individuals in the Committee of Physiology and Council of the Royal Society.

The circumstances which led to the discovery of the ganglia and nerves of the heart, lungs, œsophagus, stomach, alimentary canal, and liver, have been detailed in the following work. The preliminary observations on the discovery of the circulation of the blood were contained in the Harveian Oration, delivered by me in Latin, before the Royal College of Physicians, in 1864, which has not been published.

The movements of the heart and blood were discovered by Harvey, as the movements of the planets were discovered by Kepler, but the discovery of the law or doctrine of universal gravitation, by Newton, was required, to render our knowledge of the system of the world complete. In like manner the discovery of the circulation of the blood remained imperfect until the cause of the heart's action had been demonstrated.

THE CIRCULATION OF THE BLOOD,

THE NERVOUS STRUCTURES,

AND THE ACTION OF THE HEART.

———◆———

In what age of the world men first began to inquire into the structure and functions of the heart, it is impossible to determine. It is certain, however, that the ancient Greek philosophers and physicians had devoted great attention to this subject, and had discovered some important facts respecting it. In the chapter on the heart, in the works of Hippocrates, the pericardium, liquor pericardii, the two auricles and the two ventricles, and their movements, are described; and it is asserted that the heart is a powerful muscular organ.

The muscular structure of the heart, and its division into two auricles and two ventricles, and their movements, must be considered as constituting the foundation upon which the whole doctrine of the circulation of the blood rests; if the heart had not been a sensitive and

contractile muscular organ, the blood would have remained without motion; the internal movements of the
body could not have been carried on.

But in the long course of ages which elapsed between
Hippocrates and Harvey, the muscular structure of the
heart was denied by the greatest anatomists, as Galen,
Vesalius, and Realdus Columbus, and the nature of its
movements not ascertained.   Contrary to the opinion
expressed by these anatomists, Harvey obtained evidence
from the movements he saw in the heart, that it is a
muscular organ, and he proceeded, by the examination
of living creatures of all classes, to determine the nature
of the heart's motion.   No anatomist who preceded
Harvey had been able to discover the nature of the
action of the heart, and he says he found this to be an
arduous and difficult subject of inquiry.   All these difficulties were, however, surmounted by his patient obser-
vation of the movements of the heart in living creatures
of all classes, and by his penetrating genius and
sagacity.   No anatomist before Harvey had succeeded
in tracing the succession of movements in the auricles
and ventricles of the heart, and the action of the valves
between the auricles and ventricles, and at the orifices
of the pulmonary artery and aorta.   The rhythmic action
of the heart, as it was first called by him, had never
before him been brought to light by any anatomist.

But his observations were not confined to the movements of the heart: he examined with the same care,
and with equally successful results, the motion of the

arteries, and the nature of the motion of the heart and auricles, and the action and the function of the heart.

Harvey next directed his wonderful powers of analysis to discover the course which the blood pursues from the vena cava through the heart and lungs into the arteries, or from the right to the left ventricle. It was impossible that this discovery could be made until the structure of every internal part of the heart, arteries, and veins had been clearly demonstrated, especially the valvular structure. This had been done by Galen and Fabricius ab Aquapendente, before Harvey had attained the sixth year of his age. The valves of the heart, and valves of the veins of the extremities, were known to anatomists, and had been described and delineated long before 1628, when the "Exercitatio Anatomica de Motu Cordis et Sanguinis" was published. But no anatomist before him had discovered that the valves of the veins are so constructed as to allow the blood to flow back from the extremities to the heart, but prevent it flowing in the opposite direction, from trunks to branches. This was the key to the entire discovery of the circulation of the blood.

With that love of truth and justice for which Harvey was not less distinguished than for his profound genius and penetration, he has stated the claims of Galen to the discovery of the course of the blood through the heart and lungs from the vena cava to the aorta. There was no anatomical discovery in the interior of the heart and blood-vessels left for Harvey to make, and he never laid claim to any such discovery. But Harvey's merit was of a higher order; he was the great physiological interpreter of the whole phenomena of the vascular system— of the heart, arteries and veins.

Galen was the first who described the ductus arteriosus and the foramen ovale in the foetus, but the glory of the discovery of the entire foetal circulation through the heart, placenta, and liver, was reserved for Harvey. Galen believed that the foramen ovale was not entirely closed in the adult, and that a portion of the blood still passed through it from the right to the left side of the heart, an error which was first corrected by Vesalius. Galen first described the valves of the pulmonary artery, and the aorta, and pointed out the course which the blood pursues from the right to the left side of the heart through the lungs, but he maintained that all the veins take their origin in the liver and carry the blood to the extremities, and he therefore remained entirely ignorant of the circulation discovered by Harvey, and which has made him immortal. The discoveries of Galen in the vascular and nervous systems—of the ganglia of the great sympathetic—have likewise rendered his name immortal, and entitled him to be considered one of the greatest anatomists and physiologists who has ever lived in any age or country. In the words of Harvey, "Vir divinus, pater medicorum."

From the days of Galen to those of Vesalius, it was believed that the septum of the heart in the adult was pervious, and that a part of the blood passed through the septum from the right to the left side, and that the remainder passed through the lungs. At first, Vesalius, to accommodate his doctrines to those of Galen, said, that the greater portion of the blood passed by this route from the right to the left side. He afterwards affirmed that the septum is thick, and compact, and dense, like the other parts of the heart, and consequently that little or no blood could pass in this direction.

It was soon known to all the contemporaries of Vesalius, that the septum between the auricles and ventricles was not pervious in the adult, and that it was impossible for any blood to pass through this septum from the right to the left side of the heart. There was then obviously no route for the blood to pursue from the right to the left ventricle—from the vena cava to the aorta but through the lungs, and all the distinguished anatomists who followed Vesalius—Servetus, Realdus Columbus, and Cæsalpinus—maintained that the blood flowed from the vena cava through the heart and lungs to reach the aorta, but none of these anatomists showed the course which the blood pursued to return to the vena cava and right auricle. They did not, therefore, discover the pulmonary circulation, and this circulation was not discovered until the entire circuit of the blood was discovered by Harvey. All these anatomists believed that the veins take their origin in the liver, and consequently remained wholly ignorant of the circulation of the blood throughout the human body and the bodies of all living creatures, the undivided glory of the discovery of which remains with Harvey.

But Harvey did not discover the cause of the heart's action, or the source of its muscular contractions, and more than two centuries elapsed before this discovery was made.

The cause of the motion of the heart, or the source of its contractile power, has engaged the attention of the most profound anatomists and physiologists ever since the discovery of the circulation of the blood.   Harvey considered the motion of the heart, as already stated, to be muscular.   " It becomes erect," he says, " hard, and of diminished size during its action ; the motion is plainly of the same nature as that of the muscles." " But I think it right to describe," he adds, " what I have observed of an opposite character ; the heart of an eel, of several fishes, and even of some of the [higher animals] taken out of the body beats without auricles ; nay, if it be cut in pieces, the several parts may still be seen contracting and relaxing, so that in these creatures the body of the heart may be seen pulsating and palpi-tating after the cessation of all motion in the auricle." " Experimenting with a pigeon on one occasion, after the heart had wholly ceased to pulsate and the auricles too had become motionless, I kept my finger, wetted with saliva and warm, for a short time upon the heart, and observed that under the influence of this fomentation it received more strength and life, so that both ventricles and auricles pulsated, contracting and relaxing alternately, recalled as it were from death to life." In the twelfth chapter of the " Exercitatio Anatomica de Motu Cordis et Sanguinis," Harvey observes, " Nor are we the less to agree with Aristotle in regard to the sovereignty of the heart, nor are we to inquire whether it receives sense or motion of the brain; whether blood from the liver, whether it be the origin of the veins and of the blood, and more of the same description. They who affirm these propositions against Aristotle, overlook or do not rightly understand the principal argument, to the effect that the heart is the part which first exists, and that it contains within itself blood, life, sensation, motion, before either the brain or liver were in being, or had appeared distinctly, or at all events before they could perform any function. The heart, ready furnished with its proper organs of motion, like a kind of internal creature, is of a date anterior to the body ; first formed, nature wills that it should afterwards fashion, nourish, preserve, complete the entire animal as its work and dwelling-place. The heart, like the prince in a kingdom, in whose hands lie the chief and the highest authority, rules over all ; it is the original and foundation from which all power depends in the animal body."

Three years after the death of Harvey, the Royal Society of London was constituted by Charles II. a corporate body, " for the promoting of the knowledge of natural things and useful arts by experiments, to the glory of God and the good of mankind." Anatomy and physiology were then considered two of the most important branches of knowledge to which the Fellows could direct their attention, and at no period since have they ceased to be viewed in the same light. The doctrine of the circulation of the blood was then almost universally admitted, but the cause of the action of the heart had not been discovered by Harvey. It was one of the three problems he was unable to solve, and during the last two centuries the most eminent medical philosophers have been engaged in the investigation of the subject, and the " Philosophical Transactions " have contained the results of their most important researches.

In 1670 a paper by the Honourable Mr. Boyle entitled, " On the Motion of the separated Heart of a Cold Animal in the exhausted Receiver," was published in the fourth and fifth volumes. In the first experiment the heart of an eel was taken out and laid upon a plate of tin in a small receiver, when " we perceived it to beat there as it had done in the open air. We exhausted the vessel, and saw that though the heart grew very tumid and here and there sent forth little bubbles, yet it continued to beat as manifestly as before, and seemed to do so more swiftly, as we tried by numbering the pulsations it made in a minute whilst it was in the exhausted receiver, and when we had re-admitted the air, and also when we took it out of the glass, and suffered it to continue its motion in the open air. The heart of another eel being likewise taken out, continued to beat in the emptied receiver as the other had done."

In the second experiment the heart contiued to beat for an hour, after which looking upon it, and finding the motion very languid and almost ceased, by breathing a little upon that part of the glass where the heart was, it quickly regained motion ; " which I observed a while," and an hour after finding it to seem almost quite gone, I was able to renew it by the application of a little more warmth. At the end of the third hour it seemed now and then to have a little heavy motion, but I found it so faint that I could no more by warmth excite it. When the outward air was allowed to rush in, it did not move."

An analysis of Dr. Lower's treatise " De Corde : item de Motu et Colore Sanguinis, &c." published in 1669, is contained likewise in the fourth and fifth volumes of the " Philosophical Transactions." Dr. Lower says that " the genuine and immediate instruments of the heart's motion are its fibres, nerves, and spirits flowing through them, the action of the heart being altogether conform to that of the muscles." Dr. Lower ascribed the diastole of the heart to a motion of restitution. " The heart of an animal," he says, " bears a great analogy to the pendulum of those artificial automata, clocks and watches, while its motion is performed like that of other muscles, the blood doing the office of pondus."

" A discourse by Dr. Drake concerning some influence of Respiration on the Motion of the Heart hitherto un- observed was published in vol. xxiii. in 1702. Dr. Drake

observes that the heart, by its constant and regular alter-
nations of contraction and relaxation, differed extremely
from all other muscles. " Anatomists," he says, " finding
nothing peculiar in the structure which should neces-
sarily occasion these actions, have been extremely per-
plexed to find the cause of it." Dr. Drake being unable
to assign any internal cause for the action of the heart
says, " There must be some external cause found to pro-
duce this great phenomenon, which cause must be
either in the air or the atmosphere."

A discourse in Latin of the power of the heart, ad-
dressed to Dr. Mead, by Dr. Jurin, was published in
vol. xxx. and a letter in defence of his doctrine of the
power of the heart against the objections of Dr. Keil
appeared in the same volume of the " Philosophical
Transactions."

A short account of Dr. A. Stewart's paper concerning
the muscular structure of the heart by Dr. Mortimer
was published in vol. xii. Dr. Stewart supposes that
the contraction of the heart is not caused so much by
the influx of the nervous spirits as by the influx of the
arterial blood through the coronary arteries into the
substance of the heart.

Borelli, in his work entitled, " Economia Animalis,"
computed the motive power of the heart to be equal to,
or to surmount that of a weight of 3,000 pounds. The
obstacles to the motion of the blood through the arteries
he deemed equivalent to one hundred and eighty
thousand pounds. This supposed stupendous power he

ascribed to the " energy of percussion," the meaning of which term he did not explain.

It is impossible to tell how many Croonian Lectures have been read before the Royal Society of London on muscular motion and the heart's action.   Between 1776 and 1782 Mr. John Hunter read six, and the following were his conclusions, that " the voluntary and involuntary muscles having their quantity of motion in an inverted proportion to their quantity of nerves, is a strong argument against the nerves being the cause of muscular motion."   " If it is asked," he says, " why the involuntary parts have nerves at all, the answer may be given, that it is not for the common actions, but to keep up the connexion between the whole, for without them an animal would become two distinct machines, and one might be acting very contradictory to the other." Mr. Hunter believed " that the brain and nervous system had nothing to do with the actions of a part."

In 1790, a Croonian Lecture on muscular motion was read by Sir Gilbert Blane, and twelve by Sir Everard Home between 1795 and 1825, and two by Sir A. Carlisle in 1805 and 1806.

In 1808 Dr. Thomas Young read a Croonian Lecture " On the Functions of the Heart and Arteries."   " Since the degree and manner in which the circulation depends upon the muscular and elastic powers of the heart and arteries are questions belonging to the most refined departments of hydraulics, the author has lately submitted to the Society those general principles upon

which he designs in the present lecture to inquire—
1st. What would be the nature of the circulation if the
vessels were as inelastic as glass or bone.   2d. In what
manner the pulse would be transmitted if the tubes were
merely elastic.   3d. What actions may be ascribed to
these muscular coats; and lastly, What disturbances
are occasioned in different kinds of fevers and inflam-
mations. The cause of the contractile power of the heart
was not alluded to in this lecture by Dr. Young.

Bichat stated that the brain is not directly necessary
to the action of the heart; and that when the functions
of the brain were destroyed, the circulation of the blood
ceased only in consequence of the suspension of the
respiration.

The Croonian Lecture in 1811 was delivered by Mr.
B. C. Brodie, and was entitled "On some Physiological
Researches respecting the Influence of the Brain on the
Heart and on the Generation of Animal Heat." His
conclusions were—1. That the influence of the brain
is not directly necessary to the action of the heart.
2. That the interruption of the circulation is owing to
the stoppage of respiration.   3. That when the influence
of the brain is cut off the secretion of urine ceases and
the production of animal heat is discontinued, even if
the blood is preserved of its fluid and red colour.   4.
That on the contrary, the coldness of the air applied is
communicated to the blood and thereby diffused to
distant parts of the body.

In 1813 another Croonian Lecture was read by Mr.

Brodie, but it remained unpublished until 1865, and therefore unknown to me. Sir Benjamin never made a dissection of the ganglia and nerves of the heart, and had no practical knowledge of the subject. What cardiac plexus he has alluded to in this oration, which lay buried half a century in the archives of the Royal Society, it is impossible to tell.

In 1815 an essay was published by M. Le Gallois, in which it was stated as the result of experiments on the brain, that the cause of the heart's action resides in the spinal cord—not in any particular part of it, but in the whole of the cord. He inferred from his experiments that the sympathetic is not an independent nerve,—that it is not merely connected with the spinal cord, but that it arises from it, and that it is the peculiar character of this nerve to place all parts to which it is distributed under the motor influence of the whole spinal cord. The committee appointed to examine these statements believed that these experiments solved all the difficulties which had before existed respecting the action of the heart, its independence of the will and the persistance of the circulation up to the time of birth in acephalous monsters.

In 1815, a paper by Dr. Wilson Philip was published in the "Philosophical Transactions" entitled, "Experiments made with a view to ascertain the Principle upon which the Action of the Heart depends, and the Relations which subsist between that Organ and the Nervous System." "M. Le Gallois," says Dr. Philip, "maintains that though the destruction of the brain does not impair the action of the heart, it is immediately and extremely debilitated by destruction of the cervical part of the spinal marrow.   Dr. Philip did not find this to be the case in his experiments, of which the first ten, performed on rabbits, relate almost exclusively to the effect of destroying the spinal marrow.   "The heart of the frog," he says, "retains its power long after the brain and spinal marrow are removed."

In 1815 a paper by Mr. Clift, entitled "Experiments to ascertain the Influence of the Spinal Cord on the Action of the Heart in Fishes," was published in the "Philosophical Transactions."   These experiments were undertaken to ascertain the truth or fallacy of M. Le Gallois' conclusions respecting the action of the heart being dependent on the spinal marrow.   His conclusions were :—

1st. That the muscles of the body of a carp can be thrown into powerful action four hours after the brain and heart are removed.

2dly. That those muscles lose all power as soon as the spinal marrow is destroyed.

3dly. That by exposure of the heart to water in which the fish is allowed to swim, the action of the heart ceases sooner than in air.

4thly. That whether the heart is exposed or not, its action continues long after the brain and spinal marrow are destroyed, and still longer when the brain is removed without previous injury to its substance.

5thly. That the action of the heart is in general accelerated for a few beats by injuries to the brain or spinal marrow; but that destroying the spinal marrow after the brain has been separated, renders the action of the heart slower for a few beats.

After all these elaborate researches, and many others, had been made, the cause of the heart's action, the most difficult problem in physiology, remained unsolved.

It does not appear that any of these anatomists and physiologists made any attempt to discover to what extent the heart is endowed with nervous structures, and whether the action of the heart could not be referred, wholly or in part, to the influence of these structures, independent of the brain and spinal cord.

Haller, Wrisberg, Sœmmering, and other anatomists who lived about the middle and towards the close of the last century, affirmed that the action of the heart did not depend upon nervous influence, but on an unknown hypothetical principle, which they called irritability! Irritability was the cause of muscular action in all parts of the human body.

In 1791 or 1792 B. J. Behrends, a pupil of Professor Sœmmering, published a treatise entitled "Dissertatio Inauguralis quâ demonstratur Cor Nervis Carere," in which it is admitted that nerves accompany the coronary arteries, and it is distinctly asserted that the muscular structure is entirely destitute of nerves. "Ac primo quidem nervorum cordis examini scrupulosius intendens, tum observando, tum analogice concludendo didici nullos omnino nervos ne surculum quidem in ipsam cordis carnem dispergi." An engraving accompanies this essay, in which the muscular substance of the heart is represented as absolutely destitute of nerves.

Galen had asserted that the heart has no nerves, and that it is not a muscular organ.

In 1794 Scarpa's Work, " Tabulæ Neurologicæ ad illustrandam Historiam Anatomicam cardiacorum nervorum," was published. It contains five engravings of the human heart, and if these be examined it will be seen that branches of nerves have been represented accompanying the coronary arteries, as in the engraving of M. Behrend's, but few, if any, passing into the muscular substance of the heart. The cardiac nerves of the horse and heifer have been represented in greater numbers, and on one of the branches accompanying the left coronary artery there is represented a distinct ganglion. At the root of the right coronary artery there is also represented a distinct ganglionic enlargement, on the nerves accompanying it on the human heart. On the branches of those nerves which do not accompany the arteries there are no ganglia represented in any part of their course, but in the text, page 2, it is said " Præcipue autem nervorum cardiacorum trunci ad basem cordis, et inter majora vasa arteriosa intumescunt in vera et genuina ganglia ; in eque autem et bove etiam in iis ramis car-diacorum qui per cordis superficiem reptant nonnulli olivaria corpora gignant."

In Mr. Swan's work, published in 1820, only a few small branches of nerves have been represented, which accompany the coronary arteries, and the muscular substance of the heart is represented as almost completely destitute of nerves.

M. Chassaignac, who translated Mr. Swan's "Demonstration of the Human Body," in 1838, has repeatedly denied, in the most positive manner, that any nerves, except those which accompany the coronary arteries, have yet been demonstrated in the heart.

In 1839 M. Remak stated that he had discovered with the microscope in the human heart small ganglia on the filaments of the cardiac nerves as they ramify on the substance of the heart. In the engraving which accompanies M. Remak's paper, the heart is represented as almost totally destitute both of ganglia and nerves.

It is impossible to deny that at this time, 1839, and in 1846, the ganglionic nervous system of the heart remained undiscovered, and the source of the heart's sensibility and motion unknown and unexplained. The discovery of the ganglia and nerves of the gravid uterus on the 8th of April, 1838, led me, by a pure and simple process of inductive reasoning, to the discovery, in 1846, of the ganglia and nerves of the heart, by which the problem of the heart's action was finally and completely solved.

In September, 1846,[1] I resolved to dissect the nerves of the heart immersed in alcohol, as I had done those of the uterus, with magnifying powers of six and twelve diameters. The investigation was carried on during two years, and from examinations made of the

[1] Philosophical Transactions, 1842.

nerves of the healthy and malformed fœtal heart—of the hearts of birds—of the heart of the child at the ages of six and nine years—of the heart of the adult in the sound state—of the human heart slightly and greatly hypertrophied, and of the heart of the young and adult heifer and horse, the following conclusions were deduced.

I. That the blood-vessels and the muscular structure of the auricles and ventricles of the heart are endowed with numerous ganglia and plexuses of nerves, which have not hitherto been described or represented in the works of any anatomist.

II. That the nervous structures of the heart, which are distributed over its surface to the apex and throughout its walls to the lining membrane, and the columnæ carneæ enlarge with the natural growth of the heart, before birth, during childhood and youth, until the heart has attained its full size in the adult.

III. That the ganglia and nerves of the heart enlarge, like those of the gravid uterus, when the walls of the ventricles are affected with hypertrophy.

IV. That the ganglia and nerves, which supply the left ventricle, are more than double the size of the ganglia and nerves distributed to the right side of the heart.

The results of these researches were communicated to the Royal Society of London in a paper, entitled, "On the Nervous System of the Heart," which was read on the 20th May, 1847.

Referees as usual were appointed to examine the Paper, but none of them had ever made a dissection, or seen a dissection before, of the ganglia and nerves of the heart. Practically they were in total darkness on the subject. No dissections of the ganglia and nerves of the heart had at the time ever been made by any other anatomist in Great Britain, and now there does not exist a single preparation in England, Scotland, or Ireland of the nervous structures of the heart, which has not been made by me, and is in my collection.

In the Lumleian Lectures, delivered by me before the Royal College of Physicians, in March, 1857, "On the Nervous Structures and the Action of the Heart," I gave the following account of the circumstances which led to the discovery, and the reception it met with from the Royal Society of London :—

MR. PRESIDENT.—" I now proceed to relate the circumstances which led to the discovery of the ganglia and nerves of the heart, which enable us to solve the problem of the heart's motion or action. Soon after the uterine system of ganglia and nerves had been demonstrated in 1838, I began to reflect on the analogy which exists between the structure and physiology of the uterus and heart, both powerful involuntary muscular organs, yet greatly under the influence of the brain and all the organs of the body copiously supplied with nerves. It was impossible to avoid coming to the conclusion, from all the phenomena of the heart's action, that it must be endowed with a great system of ganglia and nerves, similar in some respects to those of the uterus, which had not been disco-vered. I felt the strongest desire to know whether, if the heart, as I suspected, did possess ganglia and nerves like those of the uterus, these nervous structures would be found enlarged in hypertrophy like those of the gravid uterus, and whether those of the left ventricle would be found larger than those of the right, and if the auricles were supplied less copiously than the ventricles.

The constant pulsations of the heart from the commencement to the close of life evidently required a far greater supply of nervous influence than had been represented in the works of the most celebrated anatomists. The heart acting many hours in some creatures after being cut out of their bodies ; portions of it contracting rhythmically, as it is called, when the heart had been cut in pieces; its movements when they had nearly ceased being roused by galvanism and mechanical irritation ; the effects of stimulants and narcotics on the contractions of the heart; the circulation having been carried on in the most perfect manner through the placenta, and all the viscera of a fœtus, which I had seen born without brain and spinal cord; the symptoms in cases of angina pectoris, and sudden death from organic diseases of the heart ; the sympathy which exists between the heart, the lungs, stomach, liver, intestines, and above all the uterus ; no explanation could be given of all these circumstances without supposing that the heart possessed great nervous centres which had never been seen, and never before suspected to exist.

I had often put this question to the most distinguished anatomists and physiologists. From what source does the heart derive its sensitive and contractile powers ? but no satisfactory answer was ever received. I urged several anatomists to undertake the investigation of the nervous structures of the heart, and assured them if they did so that their labour would not be lost. At last I prevailed upon one to undertake the task. When a year had elapsed I went to see what progress had been made, and found that he was just on the point of commencing—of breaking ground; the serous membrane had not been removed from the surface of the human heart.

On the 23d of April, 1846, an accidental circumstance occurred which made me determine to undertake the labour myself. On that day I went into the library of the Royal Society, where I found the president, a professor of physiology, and a microscopical anatomist. A warm discussion immediately commenced respecting the nervous structures of the uterus, when it was asserted that the uterus did not require such ganglia and nerves as I had described and represented in the 'Philosophical Transactions,' because the heart had no ganglia and few nerves. I inquired of the professor who made this assertion, if he had ever dissected the nerves of the heart, and the reply was that he had never done so; but in support of the truth of what he had affirmed, I was referred to the plates of Scarpa and of Swan, in which you see the muscular structure of the human heart is represented as almost entirely destitute of nerves, from which it might be inferred that the action of the heart did not depend upon nervous influence.

Having procured the heart of a child six years of age, that had died of disease of the brain in St. George's Hospital, and having removed all the blood by immersion in water, it was covered with strong alcohol; and on the 12th September, 1846, I proceeded with these small forceps and needles, and this dissecting lens, magnifying six diameters, to see what could be discovered. In a few hours the serous membrane was removed; underneath were seen numerous branches of nerves with ganglionic enlargements wholly unconnected with the coronary arteries, ramifying on the surface, and plunging into the muscular substance of the heart. These were traced to the base, and found to terminate in a great ganglionic plexus, situated between the pulmonary artery and aorta, into which branches from the par vagum, recurrent, and sympathetic entered. The same evening I showed these ganglia and nerves to Mr. Wharton Jones, and begged him to compare them with the plates of Mr. Swan. He saw the whole surface of the left ventricle, from the base to the apex, covered with an immense plexus of ganglia and nerves. It was now obvious that the ganglia and nerves of the heart had been overlooked as much as those of the uterus, and that no argument against the existence of the ganglia and nerves of the uterus, which had been demonstrated to exist, could be drawn from the assumption that the heart had no ganglia, and few nerves.

The investigation thus commenced was continued without interruption till the month of May, 1847, when I had made dissections of the ganglia and nerves of the healthy and malformed fœtal heart, of the hearts of birds, of the heart of the child at the ages of six and nine years, of the heart of the adult in the sound state, of the human heart slightly and greatly hypertrophied, and of the heart of the young and adult heifer and horse. These dissections warranted me in drawing the following general conclusions :—

1. That the blood-vessels and the muscular structure of the auricles and ventricles of the heart are endowed with numerous ganglia and plexuses of nerves, which have not hitherto been described or represented in the works of other anatomists.

2. That the nervous structures of the heart, which are distributed over its surface to the apex, and throughout its walls to the lining membrane and columnæ carneæ, enlarge with the natural growth of the heart before birth, during childhood and youth, until the heart has attained its full size in the adult.

3. That the ganglia and nerves of the heart enlarge like those of the gravid uterus, when the walls of the ventricles are affected with hypertrophy.

4. That the ganglia and nerves which supply the left ventricle are more than double the size of the ganglia and nerves distributed to the right side of the heart.

In prosecuting this investigation into the nervous system of the heart, I found that the great difficulty of dissecting and displaying the ganglia and nerves did not arise so much from their extreme softness, from their close and intimate connexion with the blood-vessels, or from the quantity of adipose matter in which they were imbedded, as from the presence of a dense fibrous membrane or fascia, which was interposed between the 'serous membrane and the muscular coat, of whose existence as a distinct tissue of the heart I had no knowledge when these researches commenced. In the most recent systematic writers on anatomy, the heart was represented as consisting of muscular and tendinous structures, blood-vessels, nerves, and absorbents enclosed between two serous membranes.

On examining this fibrous membrane, after the removal of the serous covering, it is found to be possessed of great strength and firmness, glistening, semi-transparent, and resembling in all respects the aponeurotic expansions, or fasciæ, covering muscular organs in other parts of the body. It is much stronger over the ventricles than the auricles, and it adheres so firmly where it is in immediate contact with the muscular substance of the auricles and ventricles, that its separation often cannot be affected without tearing up some of the muscular fibres to which it is attached. From the inner surface of this fascia, which I have named the Cardiac Fascia, innumerable strong fibres pass to the blood-vessels, nerves, and muscular fasciculi, and adipose matter. These strong slender fibres, connected with or proceeding from the inner surface, accompany and surround all the blood-vessels and nerves ; and they are interlaced together, so as to form a peculiar stroma, if it may be so termed, of remarkable thickness, between the fascia and all the various structures beneath which it invests and binds together in the strongest possible manner. These fibres form a complete sheath around all the arteries, veins, and nerves on the surface of the heart, and accompany them as they dip down between the muscular fasciculi, to which these branches are distributed throughout the entire walls of the heart, from the surface to the lining membrane. The cardiac fascia is obviously one of the principal causes of the firmness and strength of the central organ of the circulation of the blood, as it binds together into one mass, and gives support to the muscular fibres, like the fasciæ investing other muscles. The thin serous covering of the heart can possess little power, and add nothing to the strength of the parietes, and probably but for the fascia now described the heart would often yield in all directions.

In a pathological point of view the cardiac fascia is perhaps not less worthy of notice. Muscular structure, it is well known, is not liable to attacks either of common or specific inflammation. It is impossible to avoid suspecting that rheumatic inflammation of the heart has for its principal seat this dense fibrous membrane lying between the serous and muscular coats of the heart, and that attacks of rheumatism of the heart do not commence primarily in the muscular structure. The tunica sclerotica of the eye sometimes becomes inflamed, softens and yields ; and from these changes it is known that sclerotic staphyloma and other diseases are the results. Whether in dilatation of the heart a similar morbid change is not first set up in the fascia, and what influence this fibrous membrane has in modifying all the diseases of the heart, future observations must determine.

After the removal of the serous membrane from the surface of the ventricles, there are plexuses of ganglionic nerves readily seen with the naked eye through the cardiac fascia, ramifying on the muscular substance of the heart. If these superficial nerves, situated immediately under the cardiac fascia, be traced backward towards the base of the ventricles, they are found to terminate in a great ganglionic plexus, situated between the pulmonary artery and aorta, to the outer coat of which it adheres much more firmly than to the pulmonary artery. This is the nervous plexus between the pulmonary artery and aorta described by Fallopius more than three hundred years ago. Into this great nervous mass, which enlarges as it passes to the base of the ventricles, branches of nerves enter from the par vagum, recurrent, and sympathetic nerves. From the par vagum or recurrent and great sympathetic, branches pass to the heart behind the aorta and pulmonary artery; but the great ganglionic mass of nerves situated between the aorta and pulmonary artery is properly the root of all the cardiac nerves and ganglia. From the right side of this ganglionic mass, several broad, flat branches of nerves, invested with a soft neurilemma, and accompanied by small blood-vessels, proceed to the right auricle, right ventricle, and to the septum between the ventricles. From the left side of this nervous mass, under the arch of the aorta, several large flat nerves, likewise enveloped in a neurilemma, and accompanied by small blood-vessels, proceed to the left auricle, left ventricle, and the inter-ventricular septum. These large flat nerves pass to the root of the left coronary artery, which they not only completely surround like a sheath, but likewise cover a portion of the aorta near its origin. Many large branches of nerves with ganglia formed upon them, accompany not only all the branches of the coronary arteries to the apex, but all the branches which pass into the muscular substance of the ventricle, and are distributed throughout its walls to the lining membrane and columnæ carneæ. From the deep nerves and ganglia of the ventricles, the muscular structure is chiefly supplied. From the great mass of nerves situated around the roots of the coronary arteries and the aorta, there are numerous branches of nerves with ganglia distributed over the muscular walls of the ventricles of the human heart, and which do not accompany the blood-vessels.

On the portions of the ventricles which are devoid of fat, these ganglia and nerves are distinctly visible to the naked eye, through the serous membrane and cardiac fascia, and present a very remarkable appearance. These superficial cardiac nerves are remarkably soft, flat, and somewhat semi-transparent, as Scarpa has described, with a grey colour, and the smaller branches are enveloped in a soft sheath or neurilemma, which has been regarded by all anatomists as an essential constituent tissue of the nervous structures. Towards the left side and apex of the left ventricle these nerves lie in grooves or depressions in the muscular substance, and they spread out into ganglionic enlargements, from which laterally innumerable small filaments are sent off to the coats of the blood-vessels which sink deep into the substance of the heart. It can clearly be demonstrated that every artery distributed throughout the walls of the uterus and heart, and every muscular fasciculus of these organs is supplied with nerves upon which ganglia are formed, and which are the sources of all their contractile powers.

The preparations of the ganglia and nerves of the heart from which this description has been drawn, and the engravings from the 'Philosophical Transactions,' are now placed before you. With the dissecting lens the ganglia and nerves are far more distinctly seen than with the naked eye.

In the month of May, 1847, I presented a paper to the Royal Society, 'On the Nervous System of the Heart.' It was considered of the highest importance by some of those who had carefully watched all the proceedings at the Royal Society in 1845, relative to the ganglia and nerves of the uterus, that the discovery of the ganglionic nervous system of the heart should be communicated to all anatomists and physiologists through the 'Philosophical Transactions.' The drawings which accompanied the paper were made by Mr. West, who had been employed as an artist by Mr. Swan upwards of twenty years to illustrate his great work entitled 'Demonstration of the Nerves of the Human Body.'

On the 15th of January, 1848, an anonymous document, entitled 'Report of the Referees of the Physiological Committee of the Royal Society on Dr. Robert Lee's Paper on the Nervous System of the Heart,' was published in the *Medical Times*, and the day before in the *Medical Gazette*. The Reports drawn up by referees on papers presented to the Royal Society ever since its foundation have been considered secret and confidential. It was soon ascertained that this secret Report had been carried by the senior secretary, with the consent or at the request of the referees, to the printers and editors of these journals, and caused to be published in them without the knowledge or sanction of the Council or Committee of Physiology of the Royal Society. As no similar document has ever been published during the last two centuries, and as the existence of the ganglia and nerves of the heart is wholly denied in it, and as this Report was adopted by the Committee of Physiology, and as it would have been adopted by the Council but for my interference, it possesses a very peculiar interest and importance. It is altogether unique :

'*Report of the Referees of the Physiological Committee of the Royal Society, on Dr. Robert Lee's Paper on the Nervous System of the Heart.*

Nine pages of this paper are occupied by historical references, the remaining seven, by the author's account of the nerves and ganglia of the heart, derived from dissections of a fœtal heart at four months and a half, the heart of a child six years old, that of an adult, and the heart of an ox.

The author states that these dissections warrant the conclusions,

1. That numerous ganglia and plexuses exist in the heart, which have not been described or represented by preceding anatomists.

2. That these nervous structures enlarge as the heart enlarges up to the adult state.

3. That the ganglia and nerves of the heart enlarge in hypertrophy of the organ.

4. That the ganglia and nerves of the left ventricle are more than double the size of those of the right.

We shall speak of these conclusions in detail.

1. The author says (p. 14), " Many great branches of nerves with ganglia formed upon them, accompany not only all the branches which pass into the muscular substance of the heart." Again (p. 15), " There are numerous branches of nerves with ganglia distributed over both surfaces of the ventricles of the human heart, which do not accompany the blood-vessels." " On the portions of the ventricles which are destitute of fat, these ganglia and nerves are distinctly visible to the naked eye, through the cardiac fascia, and present a very remarkable appearance." "Towards the left side and apex of the left ventricle they spread out into ganglionic enlargements." Again (p. 16), " Ganglia are formed of considerable size on these superficial nerves, where they are crossing the blood-vessels, and from these chains of ganglia over the arteries branches are sent off," &c. " On these superficial cardiac nerves there are numerous ganglionic enlargements observed, as they proceed from the base to the apex of the ventricle, and from these ganglia the muscular substance of the heart is supplied with innumerable branches which pass between the fasciculi." " The appearances now described," he adds, " have been represented in the accompanying drawings from recent dissections."

Only one drawing seems to have been sent in with the paper on the 15th April, 1847: viz. No. I.; No. II. was sent in on the 20th May. This drawing, when the paper was referred to us on the 7th July, bore the following pencil note :—
" The drawing is not finished on the part presenting the septum of the ventricles. The other parts are completely finished, natural size."—R. L., 2d January, 1847. No. III., representing the ganglia and nerves on the surface of the left

ventricle of the ox, the author states, was sent in with the paper on the ganglia and nerves of the virgin uterus. This, consequently, we have not seen.

Drawing No. I. represents about twenty-five ganglia in the course of the nerves, ramifying over one surface of the heart of a child six years old.

Drawing No. II. (the hypertrophied human heart), in that part of it which the author states to be completely finished, represents nearly as many ganglia, many of which are slight fusiform swellings of the nerves, and besides these the delicate nervous filaments are shown as enlarging in many situations to three or four times their previous diameter, and sometimes forming a loop in this enlarged state, ere they penetrate the substance of the heart.

Understanding it to be the author's wish that we should inspect his dissections, we devoted part of a morning to that purpose, and carefully and minutely examined all he placed before us, and particularly the specimens from which No. I. and II. had been taken.

We found the preparations to have been made with considerable devotion of time and manual skill, but in many parts the nerves were incompletely divested of fibrous and cellular tissues ; still, on the whole, the nerves represented in the drawings could be recognised in the preparations ; but we could discover none of these ganglia depicted. On the contrary, the preparation left no doubt in our minds that no such ganglia exist in the course of the cardiac nerves over the surface of the ventricles. In one part of the Drawing No. I. are represented fifteen or twenty nervous filaments, and two plump, well-marked ganglia ; while in the corresponding part of the preparation from which the drawing was made, neither nerve nor ganglia was discernible.

With regard to the enlargements of the nervous filaments towards their termination, we found in like manner that the descriptions of the author, and the pencil of the artist, were

alike incorrect.   According to Drawing No. II. one of these
enlargements near the apex of the ventricle is as large as the
cardiac nerves in the aortic and cardiac plexus. This, compared with the same parts in the preparation, can only be
styled an extravagant misrepresentation.

In what we have now said we do not allude to one or two
small ganglia at the base of the heart, which are well known
to be occasionally present in the course of the cardiac
plexuses.

2. We inspected the heart of the fœtus and of the child
with reference to the question of the enlargement of the
nerves with the growth. It appeared, as might have been
expected, that those of the child were considerably larger than
those of the fœtus, though no accurate estimate of their size
relative to the whole organ could be formed. The heart of
the adult in the healthy state, the author informed us, was
not in a sufficiently advanced state for our inspection.

3. For the last-mentioned reason we could form no conclusion as to the grounds of the author's statements that the
ganglia and nerves enlarge in hypertrophy of the organ.

4. It appeared that the nervous supply of the left ventricle
was greater than that of the right.

In reviewing this paper it is evident that the statement of
greatest importance, if correct, is that which describes numerous ganglia and ganglionic enlargements to exist on the cardiac nerves in their course over the surface of the heart. The
descriptions are very explicit as to their existence, and the
illustrations sent in by the author depict these ganglia in
what we might almost call a luxuriance of number and size.
We were, therefore, hardly prepared to find that the preparations from which the descriptions and drawings have been
taken, and to which the author refers as the basis of his
communication, contain no warrant, as far as we could discover, for the statement that such structures exist in the situ-
ation ascribed to them. In saying this we do not intend to

throw doubt on the description by Remak of microscopical ganglia with grey corpuscles on the cardiac nerves. We do not recommend this paper for publication in the "Transactions."'—Aug. 8, 1847.

On the 22d of January, 1848, in the *Medical Times* there appeared a letter, headed 'Dr. Robert Lee's Cardiac Nerves,' in which the writer, who is a Fellow of the College of Physicians, and whose name has since been communicated to me by the sub-editor, says, 'There can now be but one opinion of the nerves of Dr. Lee's heart, and as an old Fellow of the Royal Society, and a member of the Medical Profession, I do think that in some shape or other the *nefarious attempt* to impose upon the Royal Society calls for a signal mark of their disapprobation. It has often, and will often happen, that papers are presented to them, which from want of novelty or importance, they very properly refuse to publish in their "Transactions;" but a fraudulent attempt, such as has been made on this occasion by Dr. Robert Lee, ought, undoubtedly, to be met with some appropriate mark of the Society's opinion of him as a man of honour and veracity, and they ought deliberately to consider how far such a man is a fit person to remain in the body.'

On the 5th of February, in the same journal, by the same writer, there appeared a letter, headed, 'To the College of Physicians, and their Impurities,' in which the discovery of the ganglia and nerves of the heart is characterised as 'a singular attempt to impose upon the Royal Society.' 'If what has been publicly said of Dr. Robert Lee's conduct, and if the report of the Physiological Committee, published in the *Medical Times*, be correct—of which I suppose there is no one who entertains a doubt—I do protest that the College to which he belongs, as well as the Royal Society, should diligently scrutinise the whole matter, and act with all due circumspection, and with that decision which so monstrous a case seems unquestionably to demand.' In another letter the same person, in the same journal, Feb. 10, put the following question :—'If Dr. Lee be found guilty, what will the College of Physicians do? what will the Medico-Chirurgical Society do?' Both did their duty honourably.

The late President of the Royal College of Physicians, who was a lover of truth and justice, said he considered that he had a public duty to discharge when he appointed me Lumleian Lecturer here, and put into my hands the identical rod with which the immortal Harvey demonstrated the circulation of the blood ; to demonstrate to you, the ganglia and other nervous structures of the uterus and heart, for the discovery of which it was proposed by a Fellow that I should be expelled from the Royal Society and the College of Physicians.

The forced retirement of the President and Senior Secretary, and the dissolution of the Committee of Physiology took place in no long period ; and the ground being thus cleared from all the rubbish, I proceeded to make more elaborate dissections of the ganglia and nerves of the heart, and to get drawings executed by Mr. West with the greatest accuracy.

On the 7th of May, 1848, I presented another paper to the Royal Society, entitled, 'On the Ganglia and Nerves of the Heart,' in which all the statements made in the first paper were repeated in the most forcible manner.   Professor Owen was again appointed one of the referees, and the other referee was Mr. Lawrence, who not only himself sees very clearly, but has restored to sight many a blind man.   Mr. Lawrence requested that all the preparations should be placed upon a table in a clear light, and compared with the drawings and the description in the paper.   'Let us compare,' said Mr. Lawrence, 'every ganglion and nerve delineated by the artist with the corresponding ganglion and nerve in the preparation.' When this had been done, I heard Mr. Lawrence say, 'There are ganglia and nerves in the preparations which have not been delineated in the drawings ; but there are none, so far as I can discover, in the drawings which are not seen in the preparations.' The paper was accordingly recommended to be published, and it appeared in Part I. of the Philosophical Transactions, with five engravings. Here is the paper on the ganglia and nerves of the heart (holding it up).

Dr. William Hunter has furnished me with an excellent apology, if such can be required, for entering into details, which the vindication of truth and justice, and all the principles of morality, on this occasion imperatively demanded.

'Perhaps it may be as sound philosophy to say that all the actions of men are directed to some good end,' he observes, 'as it is to subscribe to an opinion which has prevailed among naturalists, that in the works of nature nothing is absolutely without its use. Literary disputes are disagreeable to the greater part of mankind, and the disputants are, for the most part, condemned by the world. Yet it is reasonable to think that these disputes answer some good purpose. By engaging the passions of men more warmly, they rouse a spirit of emulation, and give a spur to inquiry.

'It is remarkable that there is scarce a considerable character in anatomy that is not concerned with some warm controversy. Anatomists have ever been engaged in contention ; and, indeed, if a man has not such a degree of enthusiasm and love of the art as will make him impatient of unreasonable opposition and encroachment upon his discoveries and his reputation, he will hardly become considerable in anatomy, or in any other branch of natural knowledge.'"

Having completed the investigation of the Ganglia and Nerves of the Uterus and Heart, I proceeded, on the 17th July, 1861, to examine the nerves of the human œsophagus, stomach, alimentary canal, lungs, liver, and pancreas, and have succeeded in demonstrating the existence of a great system of ganglia and nerves in these viscera, which have not been described by any anatomist.

I have seen the dissections described in the following important communication. The ganglia on the ciliac nerves around the iris present the same appearances as the ganglia of the great sympathetic nerve in the heart, stomach, and all the other internal and involuntary organs of the body.

" MY DEAR FATHER,

" On several occasions during the present summer you have shown the greatest kindness in examining some dissections in which I have been engaged of the nerves of the iris.

" It was no accident which led me to suppose that the movements of the iris would be found to depend upon a different cause from that which is generally believed. There was every reason to expect that the principle which is clearly established by your discovery of ganglia and nerves in the heart and other organs, whose movements are not under the control of the will, would be found to hold good in the case of the iris.

" It was on the 23d May that you first saw a dissection of the ciliary nerves of the eye of a bullock, and decidedly stated your conviction that the enlargements which were formed upon them, near the circumference of the iris, were true ganglia, and you compared them to those seen upon the surface of the heart.

" The ganglia, however, in the eye of the bullock are so small and so few in number, that I proceeded to examine the eyes of other animals and birds. which possess a greater range of sight and greater sensibility of iris.

" From dissections of the nerves of the eye of the fowl, the goose, and the grouse, you were satisfied that an explanation was afforded of all the phenomena connected with the movements of the iris.

" When the ciliary nerves approach the outer circumference of the iris ganglionic enlargements are formed, from which some filaments pass directly towards the margin of the iris ; others are distributed to the parts immediately around. Two or more of the latter of large size unite at a short distance from the first ganglion, to form an enlargement similar to it, and from which nerves are distributed in a somewhat similar manner. Thus a circular chain of ganglia united by nervous filaments is formed in the muscular structure of the iris.

" By the aid of the microscope ganglionic elements have been discovered in the ciliary nerves, but as it is requisite to remove portions of the nerves for examination no idea can be formed of the extent of the complete system.

" The method which you have employed in your dissections, by which the continuity of the nerves is preserved, is the only one which succeeds in attempting to trace the nerves throughout the iris between its muscular fibres, and in displaying the ganglia to the naked eye.

" I am, your affectionate son,

" ROBERT JAMES LEE.

" SAVILLE ROW,

" *September 8th*, 1865."

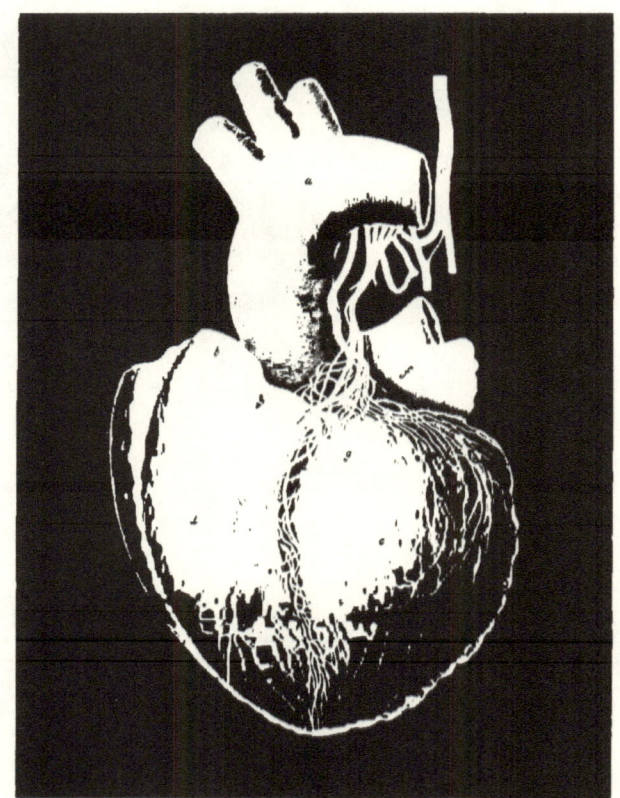

Fig. 1

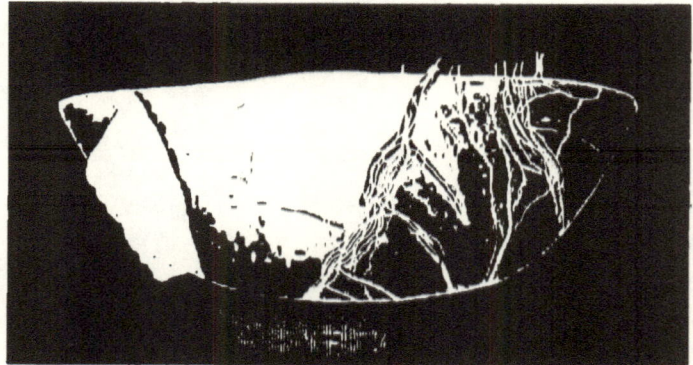

Fig. 2

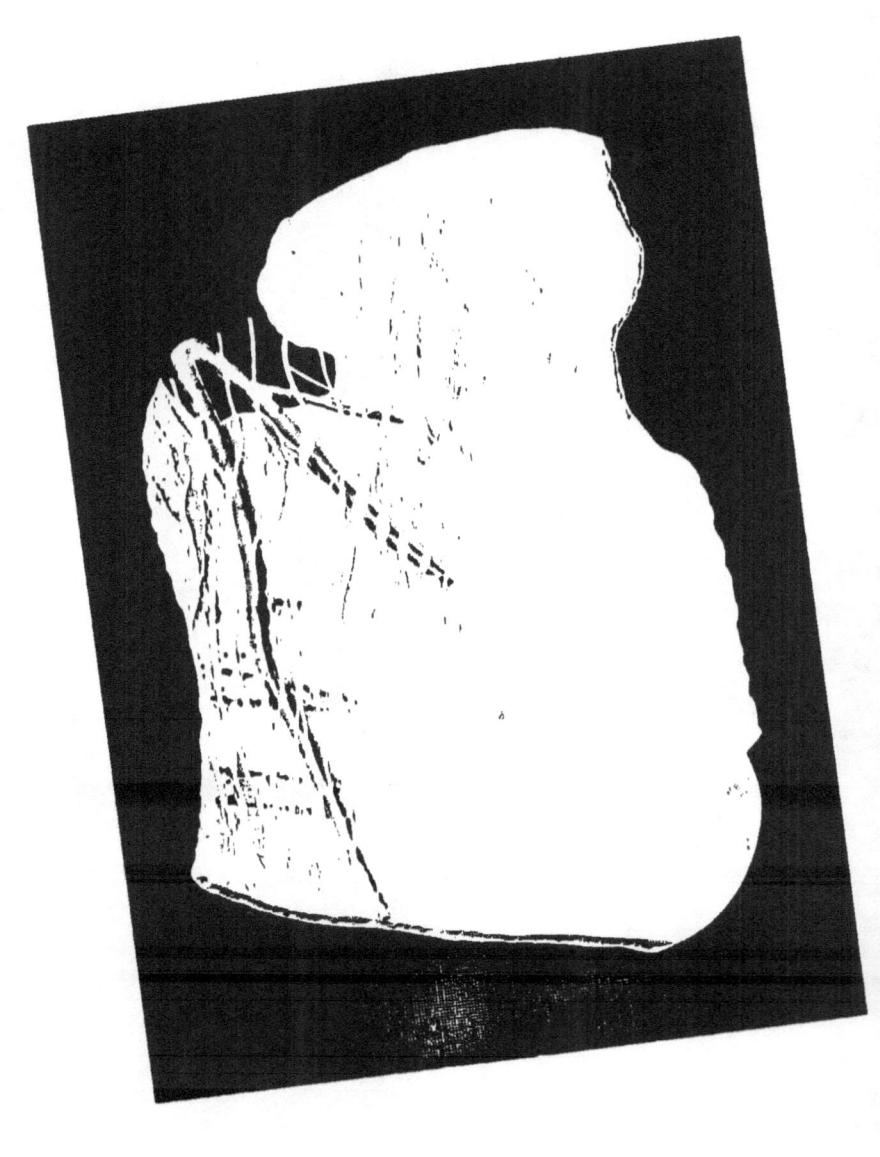

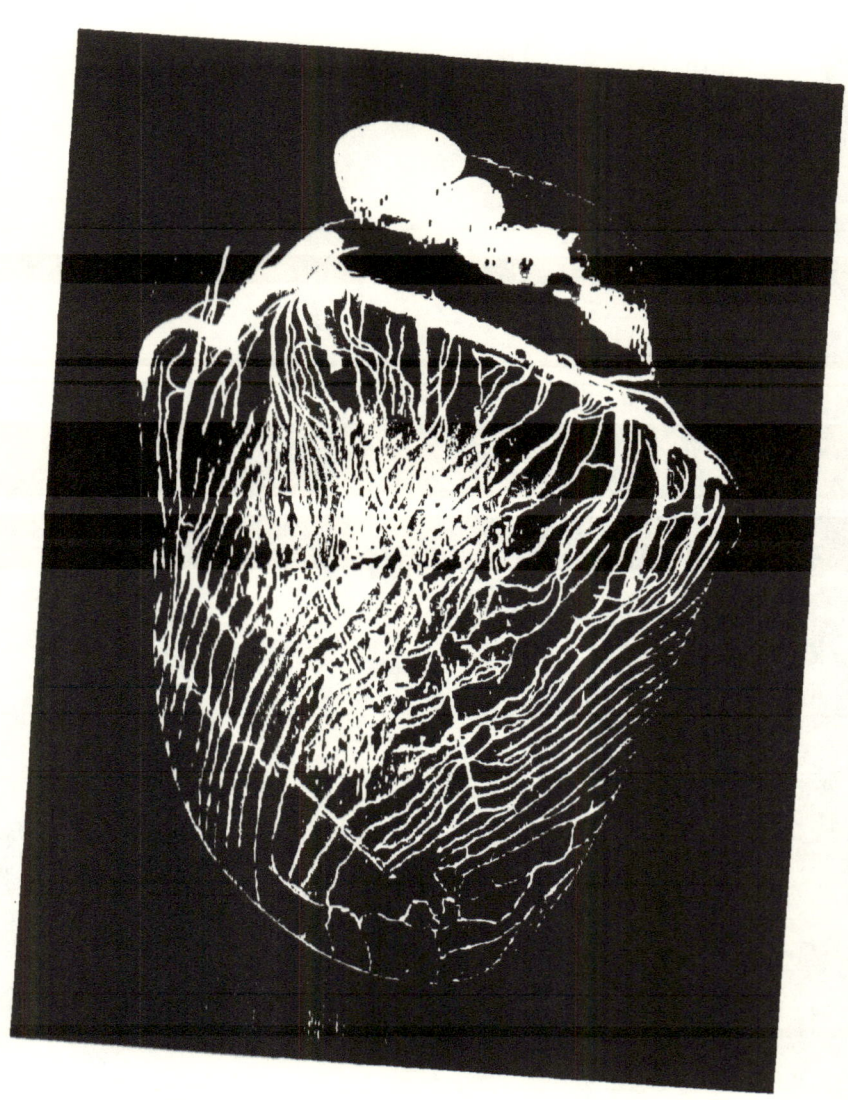

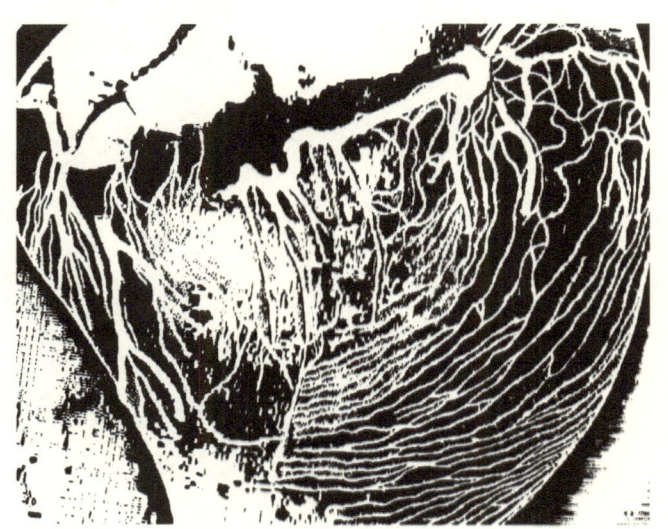

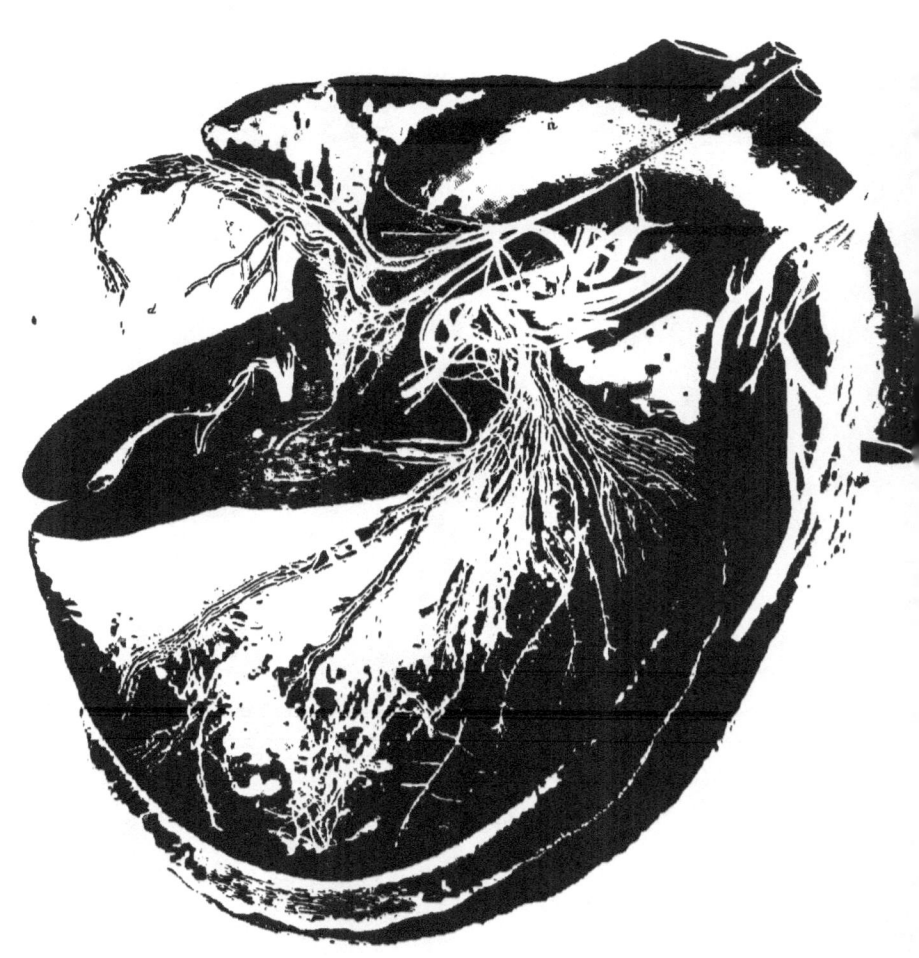

EXPLANATION OF THE PLATES.

PLATE I.

FIG. 1 *represents the great cardiac ganglionic plexus of nerves, situated between the aorta and pulmonary artery, which receives branches of nerves from the sympathetic, par vagum, and recurrent nerves of both sides : and likewise the ganglia and nerves distributed over the surface of the left ventricle of the heart of a child nine years of age. Natural size.*

a. The arch of the aorta.

b. The pulmonary artery truncated at its origin.

c. The anterior surface of the left ventricle of the heart.

d. The anterior surface of the right ventricle.

e. The left par vagum and recurrent nerve.

f. The great cardiac ganglionic plexus of nerves situated between the aorta and pulmonary artery, from which all the principle cardiac nerves are derived.

g. The ganglionic plexus of nerves accompanying and surrounding the trunk and branches of the left coronary artery, and the ganglia and nerves distributed over the muscular substance of the left ventricle to the apex ; the serous membrane and cardiac fascia having been removed.

FIG. 2 *represents the ganglia and nerves at the apex of the anterior surface of the adult human heart in the natural state, with a portion of the cardiac fascia dissected off from the blood-vessels, nerves, and muscular substance, to which it firmly adhered.*

a. The branches of the coronary artery at the apex of the heart surrounded by ganglia and nerves.

b. Ganglia and nerves on the muscular substance of the heart at the apex not accompanying blood-vessels.

c. The cardiac fascia.

Plate II.

Represents a portion of the cardiac fascia, and the ganglia and nerves on the surface of the left ventricle of the heifer's heart. Natural size.

a. A portion of the serous membrane dissected off from the cardiac fascia.

b. The cardiac fascia, with the numerous ganglia and nerves seen through it, undisturbed by dissection.

c. Branches of the left coronary artery, with ganglia on the nerves where they cross the blood-vessels.

Plate III.

Exhibits the trunk and branches of the coronary arteries, and the ganglia and nerves distributed over the anterior surface of the ventricles of the young heifer's heart; the serous membrane and cardiac fascia having been wholly removed.

Plate IV.

Represents the posterior surface of the same heart covered with ganglia and nerves, from the base to the apex. Natural size.

Plate V.

Represents the aorta and the anterior surface of a human heart which was hypertrophied, and weighed four pounds. The trunk and some of the branches of the left coronary artery were ossified. The pulmonary artery has been cut away close to the right ventricle. A portion of the wall of the right ventricle has been removed to expose the cavity and the septum between the ventricles. The serous membrane has been reflected off from the cardiac fascia, a small portion only of which has been left covering the ventricle. Natural size.

a. The arch of the aorta.

b. The origin of the pulmonary artery, which has been completely removed.

c. The anterior surface of the left ventricle.

d. The anterior surface of the right ventricle.

e. The great ganglionic plexus of nerves into which branches from the par vagum, recurrent, and sympathetic nerves of both sides enter, and from which the principal cardiac nerves take their origin.

f. The par vagum of the left side.

g. The trunk of the left coronary artery ossified and completely surrounded with ganglia and nerves, which are distributed over the whole surface of the ventricle to the apex.

h. The serous membrane reflected off from the cardiac fascia, a small portion only of which is left covering the ganglia and nerves near the apex.

i. The cardiac fascia.

www.ingramcontent.com/pod-product-compliance
Lightning Source LLC
Chambersburg PA
CBHW031320280626
47169CB00019B/2513